Me First

HELEN LESTER

Illustrated by LYNN MUNSINGER

M

MACMILLAN CHILDREN'S BOOKS

To my husband, Robin
—H.L.

First published in U.S.A. by Houghton Mifflin

This edition published 1994 by Pan Macmillan Children's Books
a division of Pan Macmillan Publishers Limited
Cavaye Place London SW10 9PG
and Basingstoke

Associated companies throughout the world

ISBN 0 333 59568-8

A CIP catalogue record for this book is available from
the British Library.

Printed in Hong Kong.

Pinkerton was pink, plump, and pushy.
He would do anything to be first, even if it meant
bouncing off bellies, stepping on snouts, or tying tails.

"Me first!" he cried when he had been last in line and
finished first down the slide.
"Me first!" he cried at story time, settling on his round
bottom with his big head right smack in front of the
book.

And every day in the school trough-a-teria "Me first!"
rang out and there was Pinkerton.

One Saturday, Pinkerton's
Pig Scout troop went on a
day trip to the beach.
Pinkerton was first on the
bus and sat in the front row.

He was first off the bus,

first in the water,

first out of the water, and first into the picnic basket.

After lunch the Pig Scouts decided to go for a hike. Off they went, with Pinkerton leading the line, of course. As the Pig Scouts marched across the sand, they heard a faint voice far in the distance.

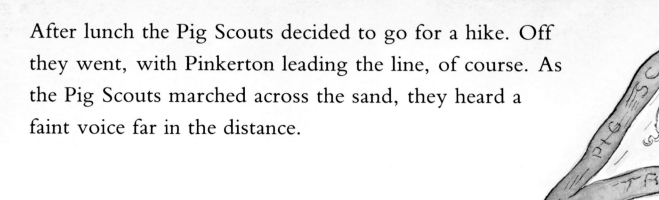

The voice called out, "Who would care for a sandwich?"
Pinkerton pricked up his pointy ears.
Care for a sandwich?
Oh yes, me first! he thought,
and he began to trot ahead of the others.

Soon he heard the voice again, closer and louder this time.
"WHO WOULD CARE FOR A SANDWICH?"
"ME FIRST!" cried Pinkerton, kicking up sand and
leaving the other Pig Scouts far behind. His imagination
almost burst. Peanut butter! Jam! Two tomatoes! Seven
pickles! A slab of cheese! A blob of mayonnaise!
A big smear of chutney. All for ME! FIRST!

"WHO WOULD CARE FOR A SANDWICH?"

Now at a full gallop Pinkerton shrieked,
"ME FIRST!"
Over a sandy hill he flew and . . .
Kerplop.
He landed face to face with a small creature
with a bump on her nose and fur on her toes.

"Am I glad to see you!" she cackled.
"I certainly could hear you coming:
'Me first. ME FIRST! ME FIRST!'
I think you *really would* care for a sandwich."

"Oh, yes indeed," replied Pinkerton.

He jumped up and down so fast his teeth jiggled.

"Good!" cackled the small creature.

Pinkerton waited.

One second.

Two seconds.

Three seconds.

"Well?" he asked.

"Well what?" replied the small creature.

"The sandwich," begged Pinkerton.

"Where's . . . the sandwich?"

The small creature curtsied.

"You're looking at her."

She went on,

"I am a Sandwitch,

and I live in the sand,

and you said you would care for a Sandwitch,

so here I am.

Care for me."

All Pinkerton could say was "But I . . ."
Taking no notice, the Sandwitch continued,
"You said, 'Me first.'
You wanted to be the first to care for me.
Well, congratulations!
Now just come along to my sand castle."
Grabbing Pinkerton firmly by the sleeve,
she led him around a few bends.

Before he could say "But I . . ." again, the gate to her
castle closed.

"All right, my pink, plump, and pushy one,
now you care for me. You may have the honour of being
the FIRST to powder my nose and comb my toes."

Seeing no way out, Pinkerton powdered her nose and combed her toes.

"Next," she crowed, "you may be the FIRST to put my
supper in a bucket and feed me with a shovel."
Pinkerton looked around. He had no choice.
He put her supper in a bucket and fed her with a shovel.

Rubbing her tummy, the Sandwitch spoke on:
"Finally, after you've had the privilege of being the
FIRST to wash my dishes
        and sweep my castle
        and do my laundry
        and curl my hair
        and tuck me in,
you may be the FIRST to tell me a bedtime story."

Pinkerton washed the dishes,

swept the castle,

did the laundry,

curled the Sandwitch's hair and tucked her in.

The Sandwitch stretched and yawned loudly.

"Now the story.

I need my story."

Pinkerton was so tired he could barely speak.

"I don't know any stories," he whimpered.

"Then how about making up something — oh, how about something concerning a pushy pig who always wanted to be first?"

Pinkerton sighed and began, "Once upon a time there lived a pig who always wanted to be first, until one day he met a wise Sandwitch —"

"Wise and beautiful," cut in the Sandwitch.

"— a wise and beautiful Sandwitch who showed him that FIRST was not always BEST."

"Aha!" cackled the Sandwitch.

She gave Pinkerton a slow, serious, and meaningful wink.

"Have you learned something?"

"Oh yes, yes, yes," said Pinkerton. "I promise I have."

"In that case, thanks for the care. Goodbye and good luck."

She opened the gate and Pinkerton sped off so fast he didn't even notice the delicious sandwich she held out to him.

He was just in time to catch the bus.
On he scooted — pink, plump, and glad to be last.